Tula and the Birthday Gift

Written by Kristina Lisonbee

Pictures by Lisa Anderson

Dedicated to my dear husband Boyd and our two greatest achievements, Tanner and Justin; also to the most supportive parents, Judy and Joel Saxberg. A big shout out to Tanner for all your hard work and assistance. Your help was paramount and without it, this book would not be possible! xo

Tula awoke one morning
As the sun began to RISE
Eager to start the DAY
Cause she'd planned a nice surprise

Today was Grandma's BIRTHDAY
And to her house she'd go
The SURPRISE was simply that...
Her grandma didn't know!

She JUMPED out of bed
And slipped into her pink skirt
Strapped on some mary janes
Followed by her FAVORITE shirt

Then went downstairs for breakfast
Pancakes PILED on her plate
Tula LOVED her mother's cooking
So she ate...and ate...and ate!

Once excused, she brushed her teeth
Then COMBED her shiny hair
Pinned it with a velvet bow
And LOTS of time and care

Just as she was ready
Tula had a scary thought
She didn't have a GIFT
Not a THING had she bought!

"Mom, I don't have a present
Is there something I can BRING?"

"Grandma loves to see YOU dear,
She doesn't need a *thing*

If you'd like to make a card,
That is ALWAYS something nice"
Tula agreed it WOULD be
And took her mom's advice

Her grandma DID like cards
And they were fun for her to make
So she grabbed some crayons...
And drew the BIGGEST birthday cake!

"That GIVES me an idea
Her mom said with a SMILE
Why don't you go on to Grandma's
And I'll meet you in a while

I think I'll bake a cake
Perhaps SEVERAL layers high
Then frost it really pretty
Well, at LEAST I'm going to try!

I'll come over once it's done
And we can have our special TREAT
This celebration CALLS for
A little something sweet"

Tula LIKED the new idea
For it was SUCH a pretty day
Great for a stroll to Grandma's
And exploring on the way!

She kissed her mom goodbye
Nearly READY to head out
Placed the card in her POCKET
And called for her dog Scout

Tula and Scout set off
Under a bright and sunny sky
Tula was feeling HAPPY
But THEN let out a sigh...

She started to feel SAD
And she got a little blue
Didn't have a FANCY gift,
whatever should she do?

She only had a CARD to give
And that's not very MUCH
Not like giving nice perfume
Or chocolate hearts and such!

She gave it LOTS of thought
And then she thought some more
Wondered what she'd DO
When she reached her grandma's door

Tula then remembered...
Grandma liked blowing BUBBLES
It helped her to FORGET
All of her worries and her troubles

She kept this THOUGHT in mind
As they continued on their way
Pretending to blow bubbles
She began to feel OKAY!

The pathway to Grandma's
was always so serene
Filled with LOTS of flowers
The best ONES she'd ever seen!

Distracted by some DAISIES
Tula gathered one or two
Then she spotted TULIPS
And of COURSE, picked a few

Spying some GARDENIAS
She collected three or four
Discovered some red ROSES
And CAREFULLY picked some more

She also saw some LILACS
Grabbed them with her little fist
And when she noticed POPPIES
Well...she couldn't quite RESIST!

She continued picking flowers
Till her arms were full and sore
They'd grown so very HEAVY
She could SIMPLY pick no more!

Then NOTICING some shade
Under a large and leafy tree
Thought she'd REST a minute
Or for two, maybe three?

She set the flowers down
Beside a soft and grassy knoll
So ready for a BREAK
Feeling TIRED from their stroll

Scout was weary TOO
And found a nearby stream
He drank some COOL water
Then laid his head to dream

As Tula sat and rested
Sunlight DANCED across her face
She was thinking to herself
This is SUCH a lovely place!

Observing all the flowers
That she'd picked along the way
Tula saw she HAD a gift...
A beautiful BOUQUET!

Grandma loved all flowers
Really ANY shape or size
Tula was now HAPPY
At the thought of her surprise

She reached into her hair
Pulling out her velvet bow
Then tied the flower STEMS
Making SURE they were just so

And JUMPING to her feet
She fluffed up her PRETTY skirt
Smoothed out her golden hair
Brushing off a little dirt

Not so long THEREAFTER
They arrived at Grandma's place...

The door opened QUICKLY
At the sight of Tula's face

Tula sang…"SURPRISE!"
Holding out the big bouquet
She was glad to be there
For her grandma's SPECIAL day

Grandma kissed her cheek
Tears were shining in her eyes
"Such PRETTY flowers Tula...
What a WONDERFUL surprise!"

REMEMBERING her card
She presented it as well
Her grandma was so touched
Clearly ANYONE could tell!

Admiring her gifts...
Grandma grinned from ear to ear
"These are so VERY special
Cause they're from YOU my dear!"

Tula realized THEN...
What she should've from the START
It's the THOUGHT that counts
When it's given from your HEART

Great gifts don't need to COST much
They just take a little THOUGHT
This makes them SO much nicer
Than any THING that can be bought!

~ The End

28498824R00020

Made in the USA
San Bernardino, CA
30 December 2015